little tree

To Lance

little tree

tree

loren long

PHILOMEL BOOKS

An Imprint of Penguin Group (USA)

Once there was a little tree
filled with little leaves . . .

... who was surrounded by other little trees

who had little leaves of their own.

In the heat of long summer days, Little Tree's leaves kept him cool.

The squirrels would climb up on his branches to play. The mourning dove landed in him and sang her flutey song.

The little tree was sure to grow up big and strong.

Autumn arrived and cool winds filled the air. The wind tickled the little tree as it passed through his branches and ruffled his leaves.

The air grew cold and the leaves on all of the trees
changed color, becoming yellow, red and orange.

Then, one by one, the trees began to drop their leaves.

But not Little Tree. He just hugged his leaves tight.

"Hello, Little Tree," said a squirrel. "You're supposed to drop your leaves now."

But Little Tree was unsure. What would he do without his leaves?

Winter came. "What are you doing with
leaves still on you?" asked the doe.

Little Tree just hugged his leaves tight.

Springtime arrived and the little forest burst into life again. The other trees grew bright new leaves. The squirrels played in their branches.

Little Tree could hear the mourning dove singing her flutey song.

The seasons continued to come and go. "Little Tree," quacked a duckling, "your leaves are brown. Are you feeling sick?"

A fox said, "Little Tree, it's autumn. It's time for you to drop your leaves. You can do it. Ready? One, two . . ."

But Little Tree just hugged his leaves tight.

All around, the forest grew and grew.

One summer, Little Tree could no longer feel the sunlight.
The squirrels played high above on the broad, tall trees.

And the mourning dove sang so far away that he could hardly hear her flutey song.

Autumn came again.

Leaves began to blanket the ground.

Little Tree looked up at the other trees, at their
branches reaching high into the sky.

He remembered when the trees had all been his size.

And then he let go.

As his last leaf floated to the ground, for the first time
Little Tree felt the harsh cold of winter.

But in time . . .

. . . something
happened.

Once there was a little tree . . .

PHILOMEL BOOKS

Published by the Penguin Group | Penguin Group (USA) LLC
375 Hudson Street, New York, NY 10014

USA | Canada | UK | Ireland | Australia | New Zealand | India | South Africa | China
penguin.com | A Penguin Random House Company

Library of Congress Cataloging-in-Publication Data is available upon request.
Manufactured in China by RR Donnelley Asia Printing Solutions Ltd.
ISBN 978-0-399-16397-5
1 3 5 7 9 10 8 6 4 2
Edited by Michael Green | Design by Semadar Megged | Text set in 20-point Adobe Jenson Pro
The art was created in acrylic, ink and pencil.
The publisher does not have any control over and does not assume any responsibility
for third-party websites or their content.